RUBY LU, BRAVE and true

Also by Lenore Look

Henry's First-Moon Birthday
Love as Strong as Ginger
Ruby Lu, Empress of Everything
Uncle Peter's Amazing Chinese Wedding

RUBY LU, BRAVE and true

Lenore Look

Illustrated by
Anne Wilsdorf

Atheneum Books for Young Readers
New York London Toronto Sydney

• ATHENEUM BOOKS
FOR YOUNG READERS • An imprint of Simon & Schuster Children's
Publishing Division •1230 Avenue of the Americas, New York, NY 10020 • This
book is a work of fiction. Any references to historical events, real people, or real locales
are used fictitiously. Other names, characters, places, and incidents are products of the
author's imagination, and any resemblance to actual events or locales or persons, living or dead,
is entirely coincidental. • Text copyright © 2004 by Lenore Look • Illustrations copyright ©
2004 by Anne Wilsdorf • All rights reserved, including the right of reproduction in whole or in part
in any form. • ATHENEUM BOOKS FOR YOUNG READERS is a registered trademark of Simon & Schuster,
Inc. • For information about special discounts for bulk purchases, please contact Simon & Schuster
Special Sales at 1-866-506-1949 or business@simonandschuster.com. The Simon & Schuster Speakers
Bureau can bring authors to your live event. For more information or to book an event, contact the
Simon & Schuster Speakers Bureau at 1-866-248-3049 or visit our website at
www.simonspeakers.com. • Also available in an Atheneum Books for Young Readers hardcover edition. • Book design by Polly Kanevsky • The text of this book is set in Lomba. • Manufactured in
the United States of America •0117 OFF • First Atheneum Books for Young Readers paperback
edition January 2006. • 17 • The Library of Congress has cataloged the hardcover edition as fol-
lows: • Look, Lenore. Ruby Lu, brave and true / Lenore Look ; illustrated by Anne Wilsdorf.
p. cm. • "An Anne Schwartz Book." • Summary: "Almost-eight-year-old" Ruby Lu spends
time with her baby brother, goes to Chinese school, performs magic tricks and learns to
drive, and has adventures with both old and new friends. • ISBN 978-0-689-84907-
7 (hc). • 1. Chinese Americans—Juvenile fiction. [1. Chinese Americans—
Fiction. 2. Neighborhood—Fiction. 3. Friendship—Fiction. 4. Family
life—Fiction. 5. Schools—Fiction.] I. Wilsdorf, Anne, ill. II. Title.
PZ7.L8682 Ru 2004 • [Fic]—dc21 • 2003003605 •
ISBN 978-1-4169-1389-4 (pbk) • ISBN
978-1-4391-0715-7 (eBook)

To my parents, brave and true

My life is filled with God's miracles:

ANNE SCHWARTZ,
my very fantastic editor, who asked me to turn Ruby from a picture book
into a chapter book, and who, when I said, "No. I can't write a chapter book,"
put down her editorial pen and rolled out her psychoanalyst's couch.
"Just think of each chapter as a picture book," she said. Magic words.
And suddenly it was raining chapters, just like that.

ANN KELLEY,
Anne's assistant editor extraordinaire, who spoke Rubyesque
and dauntlessly guided the manuscript from beginning to end
with great aplomb and enthusiasm and completed the
Ann Team with Anne Wilsdorf the Magnificent.

FRANCISCO NAHOE,
true minister of boundless grace, example of unwavering courage,
reader of Russian novels and book reports, who lent his clan name,
his prayers, and his light along the way.

VIVIAN LOW,
who egged me on to unplumbed depths of mischief when
we were Ruby's age, and who lent the names of her children
and their exuberance.

JAMES DAHL,
who never once spoke to me or Vivian when we were Ruby's age,
but who lent his nickname and found his box of Sicks' Stadium memorabilia.

Thank you.
Forever.

The Best Thing About 20th Avenue South

The best thing about living on 20th Avenue South was everything.

Ruby liked her house. She had lived there since kindergarten. Tomato slugs lived at the bottom of the front steps. A plum tree lived in the backyard. The kitchen smelled like *jook* and ice cream.

Ruby liked the rain. It rained often on 20th Avenue South. The rain sprinkled diamonds on spiderwebs and poured silver on the sidewalks. At night the rain was a lullaby of a billion grains of rice falling on the roof.

Ruby liked the sunshine. It was not often sunny on 20th Avenue South, but when it was, all the bottle caps in the street shone like coins. Windows opened. Radios played. Laundry dried. Plums ripened. Mothers took their babies out.

Ruby liked the bus. The No. 3 ran from Chinatown to the Jefferson Golf Course. Ruby's pohpoh and gunggung lived in Chinatown. Ruby lived near the Jefferson Golf Course. The No. 3 bus brought PohPoh to Ruby, or Ruby to PohPoh, whenever GungGung was too busy to drive them, and they saw each other as often as they could.

Ruby liked her school. Kimball Elementary was usually four blocks away. But whenever Ruby got the urge, school was nine blocks away: two more blocks over to the driving range to look for golf balls that had come through the fence, three blocks backtracking to school. Ruby was almost eight and was *finally* allowed to walk to school by herself. She wore lots of reflective tape—just so her mother wouldn't have to worry, especially on foggy mornings.

"Everyone should wear reflective tape," Ruby liked to say. And she got to say this every year at the school safety assembly.

Ruby liked her new wallet. The librarian gave out a shiny wallet to every child who became a card-carrying member of the Beacon Hill Public Library. It was school-bus yellow and closed with crunchy Velcro. Ruby carried her wallet everywhere. It meant that she was almost ready for a driver's license and credit cards. Ruby could hardly wait.

Ruby especially liked after school. Mr. Tupahotu's

magic class began at 3:12 sharp. Ruby was never late. Mr. Tupahotu had been a famous magician before he became a teacher. He turned scarves into butterflies. He floated a beautiful lady in midair. He owned 513 rabbits (not all at once). He appeared on TV. He signed an autograph for Ruby.

The Great Tupahotu was now just a regular guy, but he was not your regular second-grade teacher. He could read a whole Russian novel (without falling asleep) and usually one of Ruby's book reports (without confusing the two). In addition he could tell who threw the paper airplane just by the way it was folded, and fold a much more impressive one. He knew the difference between a person, place, and thing, except sometimes when it came to Ruby's imaginative writing. And he could write in cursive, even on the blackboard.

In magic class he made everything look so

easy. But everything was actually very hard. Ruby could never do any of the tricks the first time around. Or the second. Or sometimes even the 199th. But she was getting better.

She could put a coin through her elbow.

She could cut a string into two pieces and then turn it back into one piece.

She could hypnotize a handkerchief and make it obey.

She could almost make a coin stand up just by blowing on it.

She could make knots disappear... usually.

And she could make flowers appear ... sometimes.

Ruby starred in her very own backyard magic show, Ruby's Magic Madness. And neighbors on 20th Avenue South agreed that she was truly amazing.

Ruby liked her neighbors. Wally lived across the street. Before that he'd lived in Hong Kong. Wally was the only child Ruby knew who could speak Cantonese without having gone to Chinese school. He was fluent, Ruby's mother said, which meant that he could speak Chinese all day without running out of words. Ruby was very impressed. Still, she was glad when Wally did not sign up for magic class. With a little help from Ruby, he had signed up for Bonsai Club.

Tiger was Ruby's best friend. He lived two blocks away, but it felt like he lived next door. He was faster than e-mail. "Don't break the speed limit!" his mother always called after him. He was also fast at making friends. With just the right smile, he was always saying hi and having a chat. Ruby didn't make friends so quickly. She liked her old friends best.

"You never know when a new friend might become *another* best friend," Tiger told Ruby. "Just smile and look them smack in the eye."

But the very best thing about living on 20th Avenue South was Oscar. Oscar was Ruby's baby brother. When he was brand-new, he felt as solid as wrapped tuna from the Pike Place Market and smelled like fresh-baked *daan taht*. He was more beautiful than Ruby had imagined. She had waited a very long time for him. And when he came home from the hospital, she had nearly forgotten that she had wished for a puppy.

The second very best thing about living on 20th Avenue South was Emma. Emma had the cutest, sweetest little dog. He had a mouthful of pointy teeth and little feet with toenails that went *dop-dop-dop* wherever he went. His name was Elwyn and he was bilingual. He obeyed commands in Cantonese (thanks to Wally) and in English. He'd graduated summa cum laude from dog obedience school, and so had Emma. Emma was very proud of Elwyn. And Elwyn was happy to be the only dog on 20th Avenue South.

But Emma also had a baby brother. When he was brand-new, he, too, felt like wrapped fish and smelled like something freshly baked. Sam was more beautiful than Emma had imagined. She had waited a very long time for him. And when he arrived, she and Ruby became as close as sisters.

Sam weighed 8 pounds, 10 ounces, at birth.

So did Oscar.

Sam scored a 9.5 out of a perfect 10 on his Apgar test.

So did Oscar.

Sam could tell when it was lunchtime.

So could Oscar.

When Sam was only two days old, he smiled at Emma.

"It's just gas," Ruby had explained. "It says here that if babies smile before four weeks old, it's only because of gas."

That's what the baby book said. But Emma didn't believe it. Emma smiled at Sam. And Sam smiled back. Ruby saw it with her very own eyes. She had to think fast.

She climbed their plum tree, but Oscar wasn't watching.

Time out.

So she climbed back down.

She took a bathroom break.

When she came back, she tried some jokes.

A feather.

Funny faces.

But all Oscar did was cry and sleep.

Ruby wanted to cry too. Waiting for a stinky baby brother to smile was harder than waiting for morning recess at school.

Finally, Oscar smiled at Ruby, and he was still only two days old.

Before long Sam rolled over.

So did Oscar.

Sam sat up.

So did Oscar.

Sam cut his first tooth.

So did Oscar.

Sam said his first word.

"Da," he said.

Emma beamed.

"Da da da," he said. In case nobody heard, he said it louder, *"Da da da!"*

Ruby looked at Oscar.

Oscar looked at Ruby.

Oscar really was the cutest little brother on 20th Avenue South. He had headlight eyes, a drippy tongue, and a runny little nose. Ruby liked doing her magic tricks for Oscar, who cooed and drooled and clapped under their plum tree. Ruby's magic show had many fans, but Oscar was the best one of all. When everyone else went home, Oscar was still there. Oscar loved Ruby. And Ruby loved Oscar.

But Oscar was not *producing*, as Emma had delicately put it.

"Please," Ruby pleaded. "Say something. . . . Anything."

Oscar put all his toes in his mouth.

He blew bubbles through his lips.

He laughed.

To make matters worse, Sam said his second word. And then his third. And his fourth. Soon, he said what sounded like the longest sentence Ruby had ever heard.

"Da dee a ma mi haba bee dee bee bee," he said.

"Daddy and Mommy have a pretty baby," Emma translated triumphantly.

So Ruby tried candy.

And presents.

She promised fireworks.

She tried hypnosis.

Desperate, she asked for advice.

"Sorry," said the lady at the dog obedience school, giving Oscar the once-over in his puppy suit. "He has to be a *real* puppy."

"Every baby develops at his own rate," Mr. Tupahotu gently told Ruby. "You can't hurry nature."

So Ruby tried the library. She borrowed language tapes and videos.

She put Oscar in front of the mirror. She moved his lips. He moved his hips. Ruby was a convincing ventriloquist. And Oscar was ready for his nap.

Ruby was close to tears. Oscar gave Ruby a yawn. And a burp.

But Oscar did not say boo.

That night Ruby dreamed that Oscar was making a speech.

"My fellow babies...," Oscar began.

Millions were transfixed. When Oscar finished, the

applause was thunderous and utterly trans-porting. Ruby clapped loudest of all.

The next morning Ruby ran straight to Oscar's room. But Oscar the Orator was nowhere to be seen. It was just the same old Oscar. And Ruby felt her love for him getting thin around the edges.

Now the worst thing about living on 20th Avenue South was Oscar. Oscar was not talk-ing. If only Oscar would say something—*one* word—everything would be right again. Rain would fall. Slugs would ooze. Plums would grow. It was all Ruby wanted. It was all she could think of. She wished for it with her cigar box full of old birthday candles and Thanksgiving wishbones. And just before falling asleep, she wished for it upon all the stars in the sky.

2

Ruby's Magic Madness

One day, when Ruby was busy, Oscar spoke.

"See," he peeped. "Seeeeeeee."

His words were glass-noodle clear.

Ruby froze.

"See," Oscar repeated. "Seeeeee." He pointed at Ruby's sleeve where she had hidden her coin for Ruby's Vanishing Quarter trick.

Ruby could not remember what she was doing. *Clink!* A shiny quarter fell out of her sleeve and rolled away.

Everyone laughed. Ruby's audience thought

Oscar was very funny. Oscar clapped and blew bubbles through his lips. Everyone laughed again.

Almost everyone, that is. Ruby did not laugh.

Ruby moved on to her next trick, Magnetic Ruby, in which a spoon sticks to Ruby's hand as though she is magnetic.

"See," Oscar said. "Seeeeee Bee!" "Bee" was Oscar's second word (He could not quite say "Ruby."). And he pointed right at where she was holding the spoon.

The crowd roared. Plums dropped from the tree. Oscar clapped. He was very clever. Now everyone could see that "Bee's" finger was secretly bent around the spoon.

Ruby closed her eyes. She wished with all her magical powers that she could make Oscar disappear.

But when she opened her eyes, he was still there.

The next day Ruby did her tricks faster. And trickier. She sprinkled magic dust. And she said the magic Cantonese words, "*Sic faan! Sic faan!*"—which means "Eat rice! Eat rice!" Ruby couldn't think of any Cantonese or English words more magical than that. She waved her arms. She flapped her cape.

Ruby held her breath. The tree held its plums. It was so quiet, you could hear someone's TV through an open window. Everyone turned to look at Oscar. But Oscar was holding his breath too, his cheeks inflated like balloons.

Everyone clapped for Ruby, who was again truly amazing on 20th Avenue South. Ruby was so pleased she gave an encore, performing her very special Knot in Hand trick. Everyone was mesmerized. Everyone that is, except Oscar.

"See Bee," Oscar peeped. He made a fist like Ruby's, then pointed at it with his other hand to show where the knot was. Oscar smiled sweetly.

"More!" Wally shouted.

"More!" Tiger stomped.

"Os-car! Os-car! Os-car!" they all chanted, giving Ruby's baby brother a stomping ovation.

A hard, green plum fell smack on Ruby's head. *Ouch!* Ruby was mad. If only Oscar would babble and act like the baby that he was, everything would be right again on 20th Avenue South. Why did Oscar have to *talk* so much?

Now Ruby was no longer truly amazing on 20th Avenue South. Oscar was. And Ruby felt all her love for him drying up like spilled soda on a hot sidewalk.

Ruby's Magic Madness was closed the next day. Instead of performing, Ruby put her elbows on the back of their sofa and sighed heavily and watched the clouds drift past their window. She'd seen her father do this whenever he had lost at Scrabble. Oscar put his elbows on the sofa too, and he watched Ruby and sighed too.

Just when Ruby thought she'd never do magic again, she had an idea.

A great idea!

What if Oscar stayed in the house during Ruby's show? He could be as clever as he wanted, as long as no one could see him. *Yes!* There was even something magical about it.

So Oscar stayed indoors. Only Ruby knew that the black tufts moving silently back and forth across the bottom of their window were from the top of Oscar's head.

Ruby's Magic Madness went on once again. And because magicians never tell their secrets, no matter how much the audience begs, Ruby was once again truly amazing on 20th Avenue South.

Until . . . Emma made her announcement.

"Sam can walk," Emma bragged. "Sam can talk. Sam knows his colors. Sam knows his shapes." Then the big sister of all announcements: "Sam even knows magic tricks."

Ruby could see that Sam could walk . . . when he wasn't crawling. Sam could talk . . . if you considered baby babble talking. Sam knew his colors . . . except for orange and purple. And his shapes . . . well, he knew squares. But magic tricks? No way! Sam showed Ruby his Mummy Finger in a Box. He pushed his finger through a hole in the bottom of a little box. He opened the box. *Ta-da!* There was his finger! He wiggled his finger across the cotton in the box, *phh-phh.* He closed the box. He opened the box again. His little finger went *phh-phh.* Now you see it, and now you see it again. Sure was cute. But everyone could see that it was *not* magic.

Ruby couldn't stand it.

She ran straight into her house and grabbed Oscar from behind the sofa.

In less time than it takes for Tiger to make a friend, Ruby reappeared. She was no ordinary magician. She had a baby brother assistant who could walk fast, talk even faster, and now he knew *real* magic tricks. She taught him how to blow a half-dollar into a standing position, just like that. (A secret wire attached to the back of the coin and falling through a crack in the table let Oscar pull it upright.) It beat the Mummy Finger in a Box *any* day.

Ruby's Magic Madness was never the same again. It became Ruby's Magic Madness, Featuring the Amazing Oscar. It was famous on 20th Avenue South, where Ruby was truly amazing and Oscar was pretty clever too. But most important of all, Ruby loved Oscar and Oscar loved Ruby, and they loved being together . . . at least for now.

3

All About
Chinese School

Ruby's mother was also very talented.

She could sew. She made magic capes with striped insides. Magic capes with polka-dot insides. Magic capes with tie-dyed insides. Even magic capes with fuzzy, furry insides.

She could stay up late (sewing).

And get up early (to call her sister in China).

She never told Oscar to go away or Ruby to hurry up.

She never got tired or hungry.

Or sick.

She always remembered her pleases and thank-yous.

And everyone's birthdays.

She could put raisins in the oatmeal and transfer the laundry from the washer to the dryer and wash the rice and wipe Oscar's drippy nose and water the plants all at once. In addition, she could mop the kitchen floor three times before 11:00 A.M.

If that wasn't enough, she was also elegant. She wore movie-star shoes once in a while and combed her hair every day.

And she always knew what Ruby needed, even before Ruby knew.

She knew when Ruby needed new boots.

She knew when Ruby needed just a little help—but not too much—with her shortcut division.

And she always seemed to know when Ruby needed a hug and a kiss.

But she didn't know everything.

"Ruby," she said one day, "wouldn't you love to go to Chinese school?"

Ruby had heard about Chinese school. It was held on Saturdays, which was a bad idea. The building was cold and dark. A fire-breathing dragon lived in the dungeon. The teachers were former prison guards from China. They served snacks of roasted snakes. Children who forgot their homework turned into crickets. Children who learned Chinese spoke English with an unshakable Chinese accent.

No, Ruby wouldn't love to go to Chinese school. The very thought of it gave Ruby an itch she couldn't reach.

"Wouldn't it be great for you to understand PohPoh and GungGung?" her mother asked.

But Ruby understood her grandparents fine. They loved her and she loved them. They brought her treats and she ate them. They took walks in the park and Ruby led the way. Everywhere they went, Ruby went. They spoke in Chinese and she spoke in English. Ruby didn't know most of what they said, but she understood them completely.

"I'd rather stay home with Oscar," Ruby said, reaching for her brother. She clutched him like a winning lottery ticket. "We are inseparable."

So on Saturday, Ruby *and* Oscar went to Chinese school.

The building was warm and sunny.

It smelled like apples and cinnamon.

Grandmas were learning *tai chi* in the basement.

Grandpas were "Cooking with Han, the Dim Sum Man" in the kitchen.

Ruby's mother took up Chinese fan dancing.

And Oscar went happily to Songs and Games.

But Ruby wore her most mysterious magic cape, the one that made her look as old as ten and very sophisticated. It was the only cape in which she could turn into a yellow-eyed tree frog at school and into a scarlet-bellied tree frog at home. Ruby held apart the doorway of her classroom with her strong, amphibian arms.

"Cool," said a boy. "Nice cape." The boy also wore a cape. It was not mysterious like Ruby's, but it was as red as a stoplight.

"I'm Superman," he said, smiling. Superman was practicing his Chinese name with ink and brush.

"I'm a tree frog," said Ruby.

"Are you Ruby the Tree Frog?" a voice asked.

Ruby turned her frog eyes to see a beautiful princess

standing in front of her. Her hair was as black as the night sky. Her eyes glittered like stars when she smiled at Ruby.

"I'm Miss Wu," the princess said. "Welcome to Chinese school."

Ruby's tongue fell out.

"When I was your age," Miss Wu said, "I could turn into a mermaid."

Ruby usually knew exactly what to say. But she had never met a princess before who could turn into a mermaid. Ruby was speechless.

"I have the perfect tree for you to sit in," Miss Wu said, leading Ruby to a desk between Superman and a girl about Ruby's age. "Ruby the Tree Frog meet Ruby the Fat-tailed Gecko."

"Your name's Ruby too?" Ruby asked the girl sitting next to her.

"Yup," said the girl. She wore the most beautiful brown-speckled stockings Ruby had ever seen. She was totally lizard. "I'm an African Fat Tail. I store my food in my tail.

I love crickets. I eat them every day."

"I like flies," said Ruby. "I swallow my food whole. If I eat something that is bad for me, I can vomit up my entire stomach. Then I wipe myself clean with my right front leg."

Ruby demonstrated, then she sat down in her tree. She could swing her hind feet just above the floor. It felt just right.

"Ever eat chicken feet?" Ruby the Gecko asked.

Ruby shook her head.

"It's yummy," Ruby the Gecko said. "Better than bear claws. Nice crunch. Sometimes they serve it here."

Miss Wu began the day's lessons.

But all Ruby could think of was snacktime. She could hardly wait for her chicken feet.

4

Brave and True

The best thing about Chinese school was everything.

Ruby liked the snacks. There was something different every Saturday. Ruby sampled shrimp chips and grass jelly. She learned to eat pumpkin seeds like the children in China do—without using her hands. She cracked the seeds with her teeth, spat out little bits of shell, and kept the yummy part on her tongue. She also enjoyed juicy dragon eyes and crunchy chicken feet.

Ruby liked her teacher. Miss Wu had soft hands like a true mer-princess and wore perfume that smelled like lemonade. Ruby wondered if the prisoners in China missed her.

Ruby liked the way Miss Wu said her Chinese name. Ruby never could remember how to say it herself, but she knew that it meant "beautiful lake."

Ruby liked imagining. Often in class, she would be sitting in a tree as a blue tree frog looking down at a beautiful lake. She breathed quietly through her skin and tried not to blink.

Ruby liked her new friends. Superman was good at holding his ink brush, while Ruby was not. He gave Ruby lots of tips and helpful hints.

"I couldn't do it at first either," he said. "Just keep your eyes on the brush and don't look away—not even for a second. And don't wobble your hand too much."

But most of all, Ruby the Tree Frog liked Ruby the Fat-tailed Gecko. She remembered what Tiger had told her. She smiled and looked her smack in the eye. After that they were best friends. They sat together and snacked together and ran errands down the hall together. They wore their hair alike, dressed alike, and even stomped the same foot when they were mad. Ruby had her mother make Ruby a matching striped magic cape. And Ruby the Gecko gave Ruby the Tree Frog a pair of the most beautiful green stockings Ruby had ever seen.

Now she could wipe her stomach with a real frog leg. And everywhere that Ruby went, Ruby was sure to follow.

Ruby and Ruby got wooden nickels for perfect attendance.

Ruby and Ruby got wooden nickels for sharing language tapes.

Ruby and Ruby got wooden nickels for bringing in the balls and ropes after recess.

Together, they were better than they were apart.

The two were often at the Chinese school's General Store. They spent their wooden nickels on many things. Ruby the Tree Frog bought a pencil made in China and erasers that smelled like fruit, also made in China. Ruby the Gecko bought a pretty teacup made in China and a postcard of the Great Wall. When they found the most exquisite *ruby* ring—the only one of its kind—instead of fighting over it, they agreed to share it.

Ruby liked Chinese school more than she could have ever imagined.

But Ruby was not learning Chinese.

She had trouble with her numbers. And her colors. She couldn't tell up from down or left from right. She couldn't say hello or good-bye. She couldn't remember the word for "please," but she knew *duo jiee* meant "thank you" because her pohpoh used it often. Poor Ruby, she couldn't even remember her Chinese name, though she remembered it meant something like "beautiful tree leaping into froggy lake."

To make matters worse, when it was time to make ink for the brush lesson, Ruby could never get it right. She rubbed her ink pebble with a little water like everyone else, but her ink always turned out as lumpy as tempura batter or as runny as tears.

But the worst thing about Chinese school was Oscar.

Oscar was learning Chinese.

"*Lyang jiak lo fwu, lyang jiak lo fwu,*" Oscar sang over and over. He loved the little tune he learned to a nursery rhyme about two tigers.

"*Siaang,*" he said, using the word for "up" and pointing up.

"*Haa,*" he said, using the word for "down" and stomping his foot.

PohPoh and GungGung were very impressed. PohPoh gave Oscar thirty-one extra kisses, and GungGung gave him a ride on his back. Ruby was not impressed.

She found some rocks and put them in his shoes.

"I can go to Chinese school by myself now," Ruby told her mother. "Oscar should stay home. He's fluent."

Ruby's mother looked at Ruby.

"Please, Mom. I'll give you one hundred and twenty-seven hugs."

Ruby's mother looked at Ruby upside down and right side up. Then she looked at Ruby inside out.

"I'll take the hugs anytime," Ruby's mother said, giving her daughter a squeeze.

A tear rolled down Ruby's cheek.

"Learning something fast is not important," she told Ruby. "It takes a long time to learn a language. And it's easier for a very young child like Oscar to learn Chinese."

Then Ruby's mother held Ruby in her lap and told her a when-I-was-your-age story.

"When I was your age in China," she began, "my mother wanted me to go to English school. I had heard that it was a terrible place. It was held on Saturdays, which was a bad idea. The building was cold and dark. A monster lived in the dungeon there. The teachers were American crossing guards who had lost their jobs for being careless. Children who didn't do their homework got fed to the hungry monster at snacktime."

Ruby giggled. It made her feel better that her mother was not so brave as a little girl.

"I know it's frustrating, but you're off to a much better start than I was," Ruby's mother said, kissing the top of Ruby's head. "I'm very proud of you."

Ruby thought about how brave she was to go to Chinese school. She was brave and true to smile and look someone in the eye. She was very brave to try chicken feet. And she was even braver to be Oscar's sister. Yes, she was truly brave.

Then Ruby remembered. She gave her mother one hundred and twenty-six more hugs.

5

Sweater Weather

Although Ruby's father—an A.B.C. (American-born Chinese) who was also an F.O.B. (Flunked Out Badly—from Chinese School)—couldn't speak Chinese as well as Oscar or cut a deck of cards like Ruby or cross the street and remember where he was going at the same time, he was a great authority on many different subjects, which made him very useful.

Cars. Change the oil every 3,000 miles. Change the brakes every 30,000 miles. Change the baby every 30 miles.

Driving. Usually, Ruby's father was a good driver. He stayed in his lane and almost never exceeded the speed limit on the highway. But when Ruby's mother was about to give birth to Ruby, her father drove past the hospital. *Way* past.

Scrabble. Ruby's father was the Scrabble king. He knew important *Q* words that don't require a *u: faqir, inqilab, qadi, qaid, qintar.* And he was learning a list of 1,228 three-letter words to improve his game.

Knitting. He could cast on better than any granny on the No. 3 bus. He could cast off, too. And he was fast. His needles slipped and clacked, slipped and clacked, slipped and clacked, like a starving man's chopsticks at a feast.

Of course, he could also purl.

He knew the garter stitch. He knew the cable stitch. He knew the fisherman's knot and the basket weave. He even created his own stitch: the tofu block.

He made scarves and booties and hats. He made cozies to keep the tea warm and pot holders to keep your hands cool. He made cardigans and pullovers, V necks and boat necks. Sometimes, his sweaters were seamless. Other times, they were sleeveless.

Ruby's father's knitwear was all the rage on 20th Avenue South. And Ruby herself, clothed head to toe in one-of-a-kind masterpieces, was the epicenter of fashion.

Until Christina moved in from California.

Christina dressed as though she lived at the beach. Every day she wore sunglasses and summer clothes and the kind of sandals that showed her wiggly little toes. Often she was white with SPF 60 sunscreen, which smelled like coconuts. Christina sunbathed even when there was no sun. When it was cold, she

said she was hot. No one on 20th Avenue South had ever met anyone so cool.

But she was also mean. When the ice-cream truck came down the street, Christina was *always* the first in line. Even if she wasn't, she'd push to the front and buy the very last Triple Chocolate Bomb before anyone else could. She twisted Wally's bonsai and laughed at Sam's mummy finger. No one on 20th Avenue South had ever known anyone so mean.

"Why do you all dress like old people around here?" she asked one day when everyone was wearing their knitted things that Ruby's father had made for them.

It was a typical, drizzly, cloudy day on 20th Avenue South. It was not particularly warm, but Christina was toasting herself anyway.

"This is surfing weather, people!" she declared. "Wake up and hang ten!"

Everyone looked to Ruby. But Ruby was speechless.

"Ruby's father made these for us," Wally said, showing off his *W* for Wally sweater.

"See," Oscar said. "Poof!" Oscar believed his specially knitted sweater made him invisible.

Christina pulled at a sleeve here, poked at a hat there. She squeezed a mitten and snapped a sock. Then she spun Oscar completely around.

"You're not invisible!" she taunted. "And there's nothing magical about an ugly sweater."

"Sweaters," Christina continued, "are for old people."

"*Not!*" shouted Oscar, and he began to cry.

A hush fell over 20th Avenue South.

Nobody moved.

Nobody knew what to say.

Ruby could feel herself getting warm. Drums pounded inside her chest. Her hands balled into fists. Then she felt absolutely hot. She was hotter than microwave popcorn.

Then she popped.

"This is sweater weather, you big bully!" Ruby yelled. "Wake. Up. And. Bundle. Up!"

Emma gasped.

Tiger hid behind the plum tree.

And Christina hissed.

Then, to everyone's surprise—especially Ruby's—Ruby hissed back.

"Your father's a knitting machine!" Christina began to chant. "Your father's a knitting machine!" Then she laughed her terrible laugh.

Ruby wanted to punch Christina, but her father had taught her that when you're angry, count to ten. Ruby counted to twenty. When she got to thirty, she was still madder than a one-eyed alligator. But Ruby also began to feel very, very small in the specially knitted magic cape that was supposed to make her feel seven feet tall. Finally, she grabbed Oscar and ran into their house.

The next day only Oscar and Sam were still in their sweaters. It was okay for them to be bundled, they were the little kids. It was foggy on 20th Avenue South and a bit chilly, but no one said a word about how cold they felt without their knitted things on.

"Surfing weather, isn't it?" Emma shivered.

"O-only on the Internet," Ruby chattered.

It was time for Ruby's magic show, but Ruby was frozen. And so was all of her hocus-pocus. Emma and Tiger tried to keep warm by playing tag. Wally tried thinking warm thoughts. But after a while everyone just huddled together. And Christina didn't once come out of her house.

Christina did not come out the next day either. Or the day after that. Or for the entire next week. No one missed her. No one said her name, not even once. It was almost as if she had never moved there in the first place.

One by one, the knits came back out. Emma's scarf. Tiger's mittens. Wally's *W* sweater. And Ruby felt tall enough again in her specially knitted magic cape to try out a new trick: Ruby's Tahitian Escape. Ruby put Oscar into a box marked for Bora Bora. She closed the lid very carefully . . . stuck on lots of stamps . . . turned it around three times . . . then, with her magic wand tapped the box . . . and poof! Oscar jumped out—wiggling in a little grass skirt!

The applause was thunderous and utterly transporting.

Just as Ruby's father's knitwear was becoming the rage once again on 20th Avenue South, Ruby got the news. "Christina's very sick," Ruby's father said. "Her mother says she's in the hospital with pneumonia."

Ruby tried very hard not to smile. She tried very, very hard not to do a back somersault. She concentrated on looking sad. But she felt so happy, she could hardly stand it. Just when Ruby thought she would die if she didn't do a handspring, her father said, "Let's take her one of these." He was holding one of his knitted blankets. It had a mermaid on it, with a green and blue and orange tail—more beautiful than any mermaid Ruby's father had ever made.

"No!" Ruby cried. "I'll give you one hundred and twenty-seven hugs!"

"I'll take the hugs anytime," Ruby's father replied, squeezing Ruby close.

"She's mean," Ruby blurted. "She doesn't deserve it. She said your knitted things were ugly. . . . She even called you a knitting machine. . . . How can you give her a blanket?" Ruby demanded, catching her breath.

"But everybody needs a blanket," her father said.

"Christina doesn't," Ruby insisted.

"Maybe Christina especially does," Ruby's father said.

Christina was very, very sick. She only opened her eyes for a second when Ruby's father put the blanket on top of her. She looked small in her big hospital bed. Ruby did

not actually see this with her own eyes
because children shorter than the top elevator
buttons were not allowed to visit the hospital,
but she knew it was true because her father
said so.

And when Ruby finished her news
conference with her friends on 20th Avenue
South, a hush fell over the audience.

6

Everybody Needs a Blanket

On 20th Avenue South all the plums had fallen off the tree in Ruby and Oscar's backyard.

All the moon cakes that Ruby's pohpoh had made for the Midautumn Festival had been eaten.

Wally's bonsai were growing like bushes.

Tiger was pushing the speed limit in his new sneakers.

Emma and Elwyn had returned to dog obedience school for a graduate-level course, Advanced Charm 505.

Sam added Mummy Foot in a Shoe Box to his repertoire.

Ruby's mother was sewing costumes for trick-or-treating. Ruby and Ruby wanted to be beautiful twin lakes. Oscar wanted to be Elwyn. And Elwyn was going as Oscar.

And Ruby's father was now learning four-letter words for Scrabble.

But most exciting of all, no other avenue had a bully with one foot in the grave. No other children felt as hopeful as those on 20th Avenue South that all bad things would soon come to an end. It was all they could do not to sing "Ding Dong the Witch Is Dead" in front of their parents.

Every day at school a different class made get-well cards and egg-carton-and-pipe-cleaner-tissue flowers for Christina. Grown-ups talked in hushed tones, or their voices crashed like plates to the floor. No one was allowed to sneeze. Or cough. And Christina's mother's station wagon was never home.

Somehow, Ruby's Magic Madness was not the same either. Ruby seemed to move in slow motion. Even with Oscar's help, something was missing. What was it? Was it that Christina's untimely laughs and coughs and claps had added a touch of suspense to the show? Ruby could hardly help it—she wished her back. It was only a half wish, she told herself, so it didn't really count.

But after Thanksgiving, Ruby's half wish—*gasp*—came true.

Christina reappeared.

Were it not for the mermaid blanket wrapped around her, no one would have recognized Christina. She was not the same. She looked smaller than she had before. She waved from her bedroom window and smiled weakly.

Suddenly, Wally's tooth hurt. Emma chewed the end of her pigtail. For the first

time, Tiger did not smile or look Christina
smack in the eye.

Sam held Emma's hand.

Elwyn whimpered quietly.

And no one waved back.

Ruby didn't feel so brave anymore either.
She shut her eyes and wished her half
wish back.

Just then, Christina's mother opened
the door.

"Thank you for all your cards and good
wishes," Christina's mother cried out.
"Christina never knew she had so many
friends."

Emma glanced at Ruby.

Ruby stood on one leg, then the other.

Before anyone could stop him, Oscar
waved. And smiled. He jumped up and down.
Christina waved back and began to laugh.
But it was not her old laugh. This laugh
made her look happy.

Christina smiled and pulled her mermaid blanket tightly around herself.

Christina couldn't come out to play until she got stronger, her mother explained. But she would enjoy watching everyone else, so would they mind playing in front of their house?

No one had been invited to play there before, but it felt like the right thing to do. So Ruby rolled her magic wagon from her backyard to Christina's front lawn.

Ruby waved at Christina between tricks. And Christina, wearing her mermaid blanket like a giant cape, waved back.

When Christina finally came back out again, she was no longer dressed for the beach. Although she was still wearing SPF 60 sunscreen and smelling like coconuts, Christina looked more like she belonged on 20th Avenue South, especially with her mermaid blanket tied around her shoulders.

Ruby cleared her throat.

"You sunbathing today, Christina?" Ruby asked.

"No," Christina replied.

"But you're wearing sunscreen," Tiger's voice cracked.

"Everyone should wear sunscreen," Christina said matter-of-factly.

"So why aren't you sunbathing today?" Wally asked.

Long silence.

"It's okay here now," Christina finally said. "I don't miss California so much anymore."

Ruby's father was right. Christina did need a blanket.

And everything began to feel right again on 20th Avenue South.

7

Rules of the Road

After Christmas, Ruby's pohpoh quit *tai chi* class.

And began drivers' ed.

Tai chi was *maan gwo tau,* "slow over the head," she said. Besides, she was tired of riding the No. 3 bus.

"Bus makes too many stops," she said in Chinese. "I will drive myself."

But first she had to take an eye test.

Then she had to take an ear test.

And then she took Ruby shopping.

Ruby's pohpoh bought a car coat, driving moccasins, and a butterfly scarf to blow in the wind.

Then she stopped. She looked at Ruby. Her eyes grew big and round. She bought a matching scarf and tied it on Ruby. Then she spotted matching driving sunglasses.

Suddenly, Ruby's pohpoh looked one hundred years younger, and Ruby looked as old as ten and very sophisticated.

Ruby liked the drivers' ed car. It was as flashy as an ambulance. There was a sign on the roof, signs on the doors, and a sign on the back. The wheels were shiny, the paint glittery. And when it rained, the wipers went *woop-woop*. Ruby could hardly stand it. But Ruby was not permitted in the drivers' ed car.

Ruby's gunggung took PohPoh in his own car to practice driving in the parking lot of Sicks' Stadium. GungGung's car was a baby stroller compared with the drivers' ed car, but he always invited Ruby along. Ruby was good for "a prayer and a push," he said. The parking lot at Sicks' was super wide. There were no lights or signs and no rules of the road.

Ruby's pohpoh had been watching drivers for nearly all her life, so she just did what she had seen them do. She drove in a straight line. Then she went perfectly around a corner. She signaled left and turned left. She signaled right and turned right. She made a U-turn. She even went in reverse.

And because it was raining, she turned on the windshield wipers, *woop-woop*, and the headlights, *bick-bick*, all without stopping.

Then . . . she parallel parked.

GungGung's tongue fell out. He said he would never park again.

But Ruby's pohpoh was very modest.

"It's from watching you," she told GungGung in Chinese.

GungGung wanted to see how much Ruby had learned from watching him too.

"*Gnao gow!*" Ruby's pohpoh cried, meaning "Crazy dog!" She gave him a look that could fry taro cakes.

But Ruby was already behind the wheel.

"It's easier when I can see over the top of the dashboard," Ruby said happily, sitting in her grandpa's lap. GungGung wrapped his big soft hands over Ruby's lollipop-size hands on

the steering wheel, and Ruby gave the car a little gas.

Vroom.

It took GungGung's breath away. When he began to breathe again, he said, "Wow!"

Like PohPoh, Ruby had been watching how it's done all her life. Ruby's father had sometimes let Ruby sit in their car in the driveway and "go wherever she wanted."

But now Ruby was driving for real. It was as easy as it looked. Mostly, she drove straight ahead. She flicked on the radio, just as she had seen her mother do, without looking. She never took her eyes off the parking lot. The view from the driver's seat was definitely magical.

When GungGung said, *"Duo,"* Ruby went left. When GungGung said, *"Yo,"* Ruby went right.

"Now you even understand Chinese!" GungGung exclaimed.

When Ruby got home, she made herself a genuine driver's license. It had her name and address on it. Ruby filled in her weight: 61 carrots; and her height: one upright vacuum cleaner. It had lots of other numbers and letters on it too, just like Ruby's mother's driver's license. In the corner was a genuine picture of Ruby. And the laminating machine gave it just the right finishing touch.

Ruby showed it to her father.

"Congratulations!" he said, completing a double word score.

Ruby showed it to her mother.

"That's wonderful, Ruby!" she said, practicing her fan dance.

Ruby showed it to Wally. Then to Tiger. And Christina. Then to Elwyn and Sam. Lastly, she showed it to Emma.

Emma looked at the front of it, then she looked at the back. She inspected Ruby's

genuine driver's license slowly and carefully. She held it close. Then she held it far away.

Finally, Emma returned Ruby's genuine driver's license.

"Wow," she said. "Wow."

But Ruby didn't show her genuine driver's license to Oscar. Oscar was taking a nap. So Ruby thought she would surprise him.

8

Driving Is Not a Magic Trick

The way to start a car is this:

Get the car keys. Ruby tiptoed downstairs and stood on a stool to reach her mother's purse on top of the refrigerator. It was early Saturday morning—too early for Chinese school, too early, really, to get into too much trouble, and most importantly, too early for the police to be out. So it was not too early to start heading out the door. Ruby figured she would need plenty of extra time.

Open the garage door. This is very important. Ruby's father once forgot to open the garage door.

Put your baby brother in his car seat and buckle his belt, *fast*. If he escapes, catch him and do it again, *faster*. If he hollers, give him candy.

Move the driver's seat all the way forward. This is easier than it sounds. There is a little button that does all the work.

Move the steering wheel all the way down. This is easy too, but not as easy as moving the seat.

Check your lipstick. Ruby didn't wear any, so she adjusted her magic cape, straightened her scarf, and pushed back her sunglasses.

Buckle seat belt.

Insert key.

Vroom!

Can't see over the dashboard? No problem.

Sit on a Chinese dictionary and look through the steering wheel.

Can't reach the gas pedal? Use a snow shovel.

Avoid the barking dog in the driveway. Avoid the flowers. Avoid Mrs. Okazaki's fence.

"Guess where we're going today?" Ruby asked Oscar.

Oscar liked car rides.

"Beach!" Oscar shrieked.

"Chinese school!" Ruby corrected him.

"*Lyang jiak lo fwu,*" he began to sing.

"Do you notice what's *different?*" Ruby asked.

"See!" Oscar said, pointing at Ruby in the mirror. "Bee vroom!"

"Good!" Ruby said. Oscar was sharper than a U-turn on a narrow street.

"Bee" drove very slowly. There was plenty of time to get to school. She turned on the radio. She stopped at a stop sign. She slowed for a crossing cat. She even resisted temptation. The newspaper delivery boy was going faster on his bike . . . and it was all she could do not to race him.

When Ruby got to Chinese school, she pulled right into a parking space. She did not hit the car on the left or the car on the right. But Ruby did not see the words PRINCIPAL ONLY painted in her space. She parked over the words. She was relieved she did not have to parallel park.

She remembered the emergency brake. And with the press of a button, she locked the car.

Then Ruby realized that she and Oscar were at Chinese school *early* for the first time in their lives. Ruby could hardly believe it. They had never before even been *on time*. She had never seen the parking lot so empty. Or the playground so quiet. Only teachers were inside, turning on lights and checking their supplies of toys and prizes.

When class began, Ruby showed great improvement in her Chinese lessons. *"Duo!"* she shouted when Miss Wu asked them the word for "left." *"Yo!"* she answered when Miss Wu asked them to translate "right." She also remembered the words for "up" and "down." She surprised Miss Wu by volunteering new words. Ruby proudly said "straight ahead" and "reverse" in Cantonese.

Ruby beamed. She knew words the rest of

the class didn't. She was finally getting the hang of it!

Just as she was about to volunteer to say something else, Ruby stopped. There was a commotion outside the window. . . . A crowd had gathered in the parking lot. The principal was waving her arms, and she was pointing—at Ruby's car!

"Attention!" the loudspeaker crackled. "Would the owner of the blue station wagon with the license plate F-G-X-1-1-3 please move your car? You are parked in the principal's space."

Oops! Ruby sat down with a *pfump*. She didn't feel like volunteering anymore. She pretended she was invisible. Then she wished with all her might that her car would turn into a pigeon and fly away.

"Will the owner of the blue station wagon . . . ," the loudspeaker crackled again.

She wasn't *technically* the owner of the blue station wagon . . . her mother was. So she pretended the loudspeaker wasn't speaking directly to her. Ruby twisted her braid and swung her feet. And she tried as hard as she could to look like she knew nothing at all about driving.

"Miss Wu?" Ruby raised her hand.

"Yes, Ruby?"

Ruby hesitated. "Could I sharpen my pencil?"

"Of course."

The loudspeaker came on again. This time it was the principal's voice.

"If the blue station wagon does not belong to anyone in the building, it will be towed."

"*Oh no!*" Ruby shrieked.

Miss Wu stopped her lesson.

"Don't tow my car!" Ruby screamed.

"Isn't your mother in the fan dancing

class?" Miss Wu asked. "I'll call her right away and have her move it."

"*No!*" Ruby cried.

Miss Wu stopped dead in her tracks.

"I mean, I—I—I don't want to trouble you," Ruby stammered.

"No trouble at all," Miss Wu said, smiling.

"I mean, I—I—I have to go get her," Ruby insisted.

Miss Wu reached for the intercom.

"My mom's at home!" Ruby blurted. "And she can't get here!"

Miss Wu shook her head. "What?"

"I have her keys!" Ruby pulled out her mother's keys and showed them to Miss Wu.

"Ruby drove this morning," Superman piped up. He had arrived early at Chinese school too because his mother was a teacher. "I saw her."

"She was great," added Ruby the Fat-tailed

Gecko, who had gotten a ride with Superman. "She didn't hit a thing!"

"You are *kidding*, aren't you?" Miss Wu had turned a strange seaweed green.

But there was no time to explain. Ruby bolted out of the classroom and headed for the parking lot as fast as she could, with everyone following close behind. Outside, Miss Wu steadied herself on Ruby's car.

"I'll call your mother," said Mrs. Wong, the principal, in a thin voice. She looked wobbly too, and she was no longer in such a hurry to get her parking space.

Faster than Ruby could check her rearview mirror, Ruby's mother *and* Ruby's father were at Chinese school. Ruby's father had already called the police when they discovered their car gone and their kids missing, but now he let loose a string of four-letter words (bad ones) that he had memorized for Scrabble.

"Ruby!" he said, catching his breath. "A car is not a toy. Driving is not a magic trick."

Ruby looked at her toes.

Ruby's father pointed at Oscar.

"And you!" he shouted. "Her partner in crime!"

Ruby's father's eyes were red and his face purple. Ruby had never seen him like this before. She wished she could just put the car in reverse and start the day over again. Oscar tried disappearing under their car.

"I—I—," Ruby began. She wanted to apologize. But only tears came out. And whenever Ruby cried, Oscar cried louder.

Ruby's mother said nothing, but she wrapped her arms around her children.

Ruby's father steadied himself on the car. He took a deep breath. "Thank God you're both okay," he said. Then he wrapped his arms around his family.

That night after they said their prayers, Ruby's mother and father held their children just a little longer. They told them how much they loved them. And they asked if they had learned their lesson.

"Yes," Ruby replied, climbing into bed.

Ruby felt different. Something *had* changed. But she couldn't quite put her elbow on it. Her bed was warm. Her pillow was soft. Her belly was full.

"Yes," Oscar echoed Ruby. But that was all he said. His eyelids floated down like window shades. His smile hung in the air, and then he was fast asleep in his father's arms.

Their father carried Oscar into the nursery and tucked him in. There was the sound of kisses planted on foreheads. Then the sound of slippered footsteps across the floor. Quietly, a light turned off. Then another.

Ruby and Oscar had had a very long day. And so had their mother and father. They would all talk about lessons learned tomorrow.

Just as they were about to close Ruby's door and turn everything into yesterday, Ruby got it.

"I learned," she whispered, her voice slipping into dreams, "never to park in the principal's space."

9

Welcome to America!

Ruby was famous.

But still, she had to clean her room.

Her picture had appeared on the front page of the *Beacon Hill News*, with the headline JUNIOR JOYRIDER DRIVES FOUR BLOCKS TO CHINESE SCHOOL. There was a picture of her genuine driver's license. And Oscar was mentioned, but only once in the third paragraph.

Oscar was not famous.

But still, Oscar did *not* have to clean his room.

It wasn't fair.

Ruby was not exactly a good cleaner-upper.

She found magic tricks she had long forgotten, which, of course, needed lots of practice.

And chapter books she had to reread—right away.

She found her frog-leg tights and pulled them on . . . which led to the magic capes . . . which led to the sequined shoes . . . which led to the jingly handbag . . . which led to every single thing Ruby's father had ever knitted for her. Ruby was a great dresser-upper.

A long-lost roll of reflective tape proved to be very useful in refreshing Ruby's wardrobe.

As did a long-lost tea party.

The more she cleaned her room, the messier it got.

Until Ruby's mother, who was a good

cleaner-upper, finished Oscar's room and came to help Ruby with hers.

Ruby's room was transformed in an instant.

And vacuumed.

And dusted.

And sorted.

It felt like a wide, open field.

"Ruby," Ruby's mother said, catching her breath. "This room is possibly big enough for two, don't you think?"

"Two?" Ruby didn't know what to say. What was her mother thinking? It had always been Ruby's room and only Ruby's room.

"Oscar has his own room," Ruby said firmly.

"I didn't mean Oscar," Ruby's mom smiled.

Not Oscar? Ruby's eyes grew big and round. Could Ruby possibly be getting a baby sister? Or a puppy?

Ruby's mother shook her head. She handed Ruby a picture. Smiling at Ruby was a little girl about Ruby's age. She had golf balls embroidered all over her dress, miscellaneous Band-Aids on her knees, and a Mercurochrome stripe painted across her chin.

"Remember your cousin, Flying Duck?" Ruby's mother asked. "And my sister, Second Aunt? And her husband, Second Uncle? They will be emigrating from China, and they will live with us for a while. Flying Duck likes Chinese opera and knows the Chinese teacup dance. She can also fish and grow rice. You two will have lots of fun together."

Ruby had heard about immigrant relatives. They

are noisy and loud. They talk too fast in a language you have trouble understanding even when it's spoken slowly. They sleep when it's light and wake when it's dark. They don't laugh at your jokes, but they laugh at everything else. They eat cloud ears and bird spit. They get lost. They dress funny.

"I know you would just love to have some girl company," her mother said.

Girl company? With a stranger who dances with teacups? No thanks! The Mercurochrome and Band-Aids were good signs, but Chinese opera and broken teacups were definitely *bad* news.

No, Ruby wouldn't love to share her room—especially not with a migrating duck!

But before Ruby could say quack, there was a loud racket outside Ruby's window. Ruby's father was wobbling on a ladder and tangling with a hose. He didn't like ladders, and he didn't like getting wet. But Ruby did!

Although Ruby showed no talent for cleaning a certain room in the house, she was very talented at climbing ladders and aiming the hose. In less time than it takes to turn on a vacuum cleaner, Ruby had power-washed the entire house. Even the front steps were clean enough for Oscar to teethe on.

Before Ruby could turn the hose on anything else, her father was wobbling again—with a can of paint! It was Ruby's lucky day. She had never painted from a can that big before.

But painting a house is a lot of work. Soon, PohPoh and GungGung came to help, and so did Ruby's aunts and uncles and cousins. Although Ruby wanted to paint every inch by herself, she remembered to share. She just loved it when all of her relatives crowded into one place. Together, they painted the entire house, inside and out, all in less than a week.

Soon, Ruby's house didn't look like Ruby's house anymore.

It looked bigger.

And brighter.

It gave 20th Avenue South a certain glow.

Ruby's father had even trimmed and combed the lawn.

"I'd park my car in front of your house any day," GungGung said, taking it all in from across the street. "Flying Duck will love living here."

"We will love having her," Ruby's father replied.

Aaaaack! Ruby could hardly believe her ears! She felt tricked! Her house had been cleaned and hosed and painted for *whom? For Flying Duck?* Sure, it was a lot of fun ... but it wasn't fair! She stomped her foot.

To make matters worse, everyone knew that Flying Duck was coming and couldn't stop talking about her. Ruby the Gecko and her mother came to visit, and they brought a pair of duck-feet tights and a new winter coat for Flying Duck. Christina and her mother also came, and they left a couple of fluffy comforters to welcome the immigrants. Emma and Sam and Elwyn and their parents visited too, and they left beautiful handmade pillows. Wally and his dad brought over a special bonsai for the expected guests. And Tiger and his mom came with a covered casserole—"a first taste of American food"—and a little something special for Ruby.

"Thank you," said Ruby. It was Ruby's favorite dish: macaroni and cheese with little slices of hot dog mixed in everywhere. Ruby tried very, very hard not to enjoy it. She tried very, very hard to pretend it was bitter melon. But it didn't work. It was very, very yummy.

At school Ruby's art class made a large banner with Chinese characters that read, WELCOME TO AMERICA! Ruby got to demonstrate how to hold a brush and how to make ink.

In reading class Mr. Tupahotu had the children read Chinese folktales to learn about Flying Duck's culture. He asked Ruby to read first.

In music the class watched a Chinese opera video. Then Ruby sang a Chinese song Oscar had taught her. She sounded like a real diva. And the concert hall went *wild with applause* when she was done.

In gym class Ruby was the only one who could do the Chinese fan dance the first time around (she had been watching her mother). She gave everyone lots of tips and helpful hints.

Not only was Ruby famous, but the entire universe was spinning around Ruby and her family. Ruby could hardly stand it. Expecting immigrant relatives was turning out to be more exciting than Ruby wanted to admit.

Ruby loved it.

And she didn't love it.

Nothing was the same anymore. The table was set with extra bowls and chopsticks. The bathroom held extra toothbrushes. And Ruby's room didn't look like Ruby's room anymore. Ruby's bed was gone, and in its place was a new bunk bed. A new pair of Thunder Bunny slippers was placed next to Ruby's tattered pair. A new Lightning Bunny light was waiting for someone to read in bed. Everything was changing as fast as shuffling cards. Even Ruby didn't feel like herself. She worried about many things.

What if Flying Duck was actually a sneaky duck? What if she could eat her dessert and Ruby's, too? Or what if she was a bully duck? And helped herself to Ruby's magic capes? Or looked in Ruby's secret cigar box?

What if she snored?

Ruby lay awake all night. Tomorrow, Flying Duck would be here. Tomorrow, half of her room would not be hers, half of her closet would belong to someone else, half of her window would be looked through by another pair of eyes, half of the wishes in the night sky would not be hers, and half—if not more—of everything she'd hear would be in Chinese.

If there were a magic trick to keep 20th Avenue South from changing, to keep Flying Duck from arriving, to keep everything just the way it was, Ruby would have traded all she had for it.

Ruby's room spun. How would she communicate with someone who didn't understand any English? she wondered. Could Flying Duck swim, or did she just fly? Did she like climbing trees? Did she know magic tricks that were bigger and better than hers?

Then Ruby wondered what it would feel like to leave her home, like Flying Duck was doing. What would it feel like to leave 20th Avenue South? There would be so many things Ruby

would miss: rain on the rooftop, her house, her plum tree . . . most of all, her friends. The thought of going away made Ruby feel very sad. Was Flying Duck sad to leave her friends? Would she like her new home? Would she like Oscar? Would she like Ruby? Was she as scared as Ruby was about tomorrow?

Usually, Ruby loved the airport. The floors were shiny. The windows were big and the shops cheerful. Usually, Ruby sampled the pretzels . . . then the flavor-of-the-day frozen yogurt. She'd inspect the key chains . . . then the postcards. Usually, Ruby rode the people movers and—when no one was looking—ogled a shiny golf cart. Ruby often checked the arrival times and the departure times and pretended she was waiting to board the 6:55 to Copenhagen. And she loved the way people walked—fast, fast, fast.

But not today. Ruby could hardly move. She hardly even said one word.

Nearly everyone from 20th Avenue South was at the airport. Everyone was excited and talked fast, fast, fast. Even Elwyn, who barked at the planes.

Planes went up and planes came down. Sam went up the escalator and Sam came down the escalator. And Oscar found the ashtrays.

But Ruby didn't move her amphibian legs one bit. She wore her most mysterious magic cape, the one that made her look as old as ten and very sophisticated. It was the only cape in which she could turn into a Chinese gliding tree frog at the airport . . . if she needed to.

She waited very quietly. She breathed through her skin and kept her frog eyes wide open.

GungGung put his arm around Ruby.
"Don't worry," he said.

Eventually, Ruby was the only one paying attention when people started to trickle past the gate.

A little girl about Ruby's size came toward her. Ruby's eyes followed her. She looked like a duck . . . she walked like a duck . . . she sounded like . . . but it wasn't Flying Duck.

She inspected every little girl that went past.

Finally, Ruby's head hurt. Her feet hurt. And her stomach growled for a big bowl of fried rice.

And still there was no sign of her cousin.

Just when Ruby thought her frog eyes would dry up from looking so hard, something sparkled in the distance. It got brighter and bigger, like an

approaching star, as it moved closer. No one noticed it but Ruby. No one would have known what it was except Ruby. Ruby knew it could mean only one thing.

Could that be—? Was it . . . possible?

Ruby rubbed her eyes. She could hardly believe it. It was too good to be true.

It was Flying Duck! She was wearing a big smile, but most important of all, she was wearing . . . *lots* of reflective tape. It was the most beautiful thing Ruby had ever seen. Ruby looked her smack in the reflective tape.

Then Ruby remembered, and she looked her smack in the eye instead.

"Lubee?" came a small voice from inside the reflective tape.

Ruby knew it was hard for Chinese speakers to say their *r*'s, but Ruby was used to it and didn't mind.

"Ruby Lu, brave and true," Ruby answered, giving her cousin a genuine Chinese bow and salute. "Flying Duck?"

The girl stepped toward Ruby. On the suitcase next to her were the words FLYING DUCK, NEVER OUT OF LUCK!, written out in perfect reflective tape. Flying Duck bowed deeply and gave Ruby a little salute back.

Ruby's tongue fell out. After that, Ruby didn't know what else to say. She couldn't remember a single Chinese phrase she had learned.

So she threw her arms around her cousin and held on tight.

And Flying Duck threw her arms around Ruby and held on even tighter.

All at once, Ruby felt as though she had known Flying Duck all her life. Her cousin from halfway around the world felt more familiar than Ruby could have ever imagined.

And for the first time, Ruby felt that everything was going to be okay.

And everything was.

And Ruby couldn't wait to take her cousin home to 20th Avenue South.

RUBY'S
Fantastic Glossary and Pronunciation Guide

(All Chinese pronunciations are in Cantonese/Taishanese.)

Apgar test—A score, between zero and ten, given to babies at one minute and then five minutes after birth, to determine the baby's condition and reflexes. Named for Dr. Virginia Apgar who developed it in 1952.

bird spit (a.k.a. bird's nest)—A crunchy food that looks like glass noodles; a rare delicacy; used to make soup.

bitter melon (*fwu gua*; sounds like "foo gwa")—Green melon with deep ridges that tastes worse than medicine.

bonsai—Twisted trees and bushes that get lots of haircuts.

cloud ears (a.k.a. tree ears or black fungus)—Crunchy, black fungi that grow on trees; looks like shoe leather scraps.

daan taht—Egg custard tart.

dim sum (literally, "dot the heart")—Tiny hors d'oeuvres served in a Chinese lunch.

dragon eyes (*loong an*)—Juicy fruit that is

covered by a brittle brown shell; looks like chocolate truffles, but it's sweeter.

duo (sounds like "dwo")—Left.

duo jiee (sounds like "dwo jee-yea")—Thank you.

glass noodles (a.k.a. bean thread or vermicelli)—See-through noodles, clear as glass. Yummy.

gnao gow (sounds like "gnow-gow")—"Crazy dog!" Usually used as a friendly reprimand when someone is getting carried away with a crazy idea.

GungGung (sounds like "goonggoong")—Grandpa on your mother's side.

haa—Down.

jook—Rice porridge; served plain if you're sick. Served with yummy condiments if you're not.

lyang jiak lo fwu (sounds like "liang jiac low foo")—A nursery song called "Two Tigers," sung to tune of "Frère Jacques."

maan gwo haur (sounds like "maan gwo tau")—"Slow over the head"; too slow.

Mercurochrome—Red liquid dabbed on cuts and scrapes to kill germs. Looks like shiny blood. No longer popular in the United States, but still in use in China and other parts of the world.

Midautumn Festival (a.k.a. Moon Festival)— Major Chinese holiday on the fifteenth day of the eighth lunar month, when the moon is the biggest and brightest of the year. Similar to the American Thanksgiving.

moon cakes—Dense, little cakes, round as the moon, filled with red bean paste or lotus seed paste. Yummy. Also perfect hockey pucks if left out overnight.

PohPoh—Grandma on your mother's side.

siaang (sounds like "seeyang")—Up.

sic faan (literally, "eat rice")—An invitation to eat.

Sicks' Stadium—officially, Sicks' Seattle Stadium, named for Emil Sick, who built it in 1938. Located at the corner of Rainier Avenue South and South McClellan Street, it was home to baseball's Rainiers, Angels, and Seattle's first major-league team, the Seattle Pilots. Sicks' Stadium was torn down in 1979, but it was fictionally resurrected for this book.

summa cum laude—Latin for "with the utmost praise"; to graduate with highest honors.

tai chi—A martial arts exercise that requires slow movements. Looks like people are stuck in Jell-O.

taro cakes (*baak go*)—Salty, pasty cakes made of taro and dried shrimp. Often served with oyster sauce.

tempura—Japanese dish of seafood or vegetables dipped in lumpy batter and deep-fried; crunchy and yummy.

Yo (sounds like "yow")—Right.

AUTHOR'S NOTE

The Chinese words spoken in this book are a combination of the Cantonese and Taishanese dialects of southern China. These have been the common dialects in Chinese American homes for more than one hundred years.